First American edition 2002 by Kane/Miller Book Publishers
La Jolla, California

Originally published in Ghana in 1997 by
Sub-Saharan Publishers, Legon, Accra, Ghana

Library of Congress Cataloging-in-Publication Data
Asare, Meshack, 1945-
Sosu's call / by Meshack Asare.–1st Amer. ed.
p. cm.
Summary: When a great storm threatens, Sosu, an African boy who
is unable to walk, joins his dog Fusa in helping save their village.
ISBN 1-929132-21-2
[1. Physically handicapped–Fiction. 2. Courage–Fiction.
3. Dogs–Fiction. 4. Storms–Fiction. 5. Africa–Fiction.] I.Title.
PZ7.A764 So 2001 [Fic]–dc21 2001038820

Printed and bound in Singapore by Tien Wah Press Pte. Ltd.

1 2 3 4 5 6 7 8 9 10

Sosu's Call

By Meshack Asare

Kane/Miller
BOOK PUBLISHERS

Somewhere on a narrow strip of land between the sea and the lagoon, there is a small village. Some say it used to be bigger, but with every crashing wave, the sea claims a little more of the land. The lagoon stretches as far as the eye can see, and it swells up whenever it pleases. Yet the people will not leave their village. The marriage between the sea and the lagoon is good for them, they say. The sea provides good fishing, while the lagoon supplies other delicacies. The soil too produces excellent vegetables for the market.

4

Sosu lives in the village with his parents, his sister Fafa, his younger brother Bubu, Fusa the dog, and scores of chickens. Their house, like most other houses in the village, is only a stone's throw from the sea.

Most of the things Sosu knows about the village are from the days when he was small enough to be carried around on his mother's back. That was a long time ago, when everyone wished for him to stand up on his legs and walk. But that did not happen.

For many years, he only saw the world from behind his family's fence.

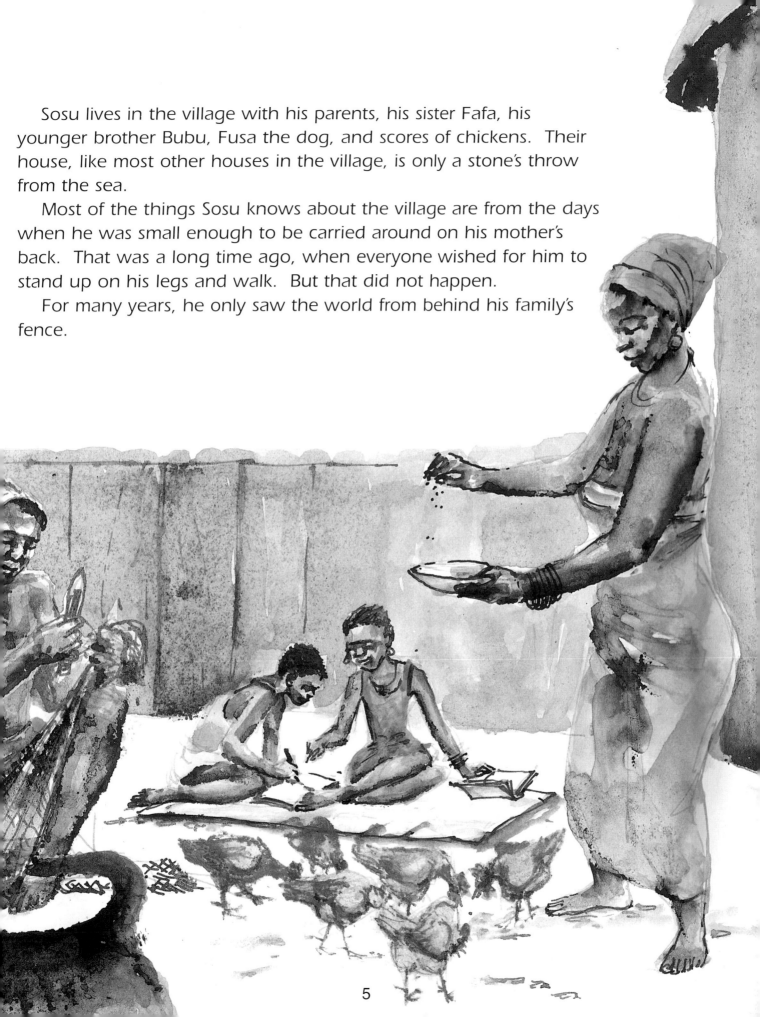

In the mornings, Sosu would sit by the gate, watching as everyone left for the day. Ma and Da were the first to go. Fafa and Bubu followed shortly, off to school, with Fusa the dog running after them.

The dog always returned, panting, his eyes shining with the satisfaction of having been outside. It was this, more than anything else, which made Sosu envious. "What use is a boy without a pair of good, strong legs?" he thought.

Everyone cared for Sosu. Da in particular did everything possible to make him feel like a normal boy. He taught Sosu to repair broken fishing nets, taking him in his small canoe to paddle and fish in the lagoon.

But one day while fishing with Da, two stern-looking men drew up alongside Da's canoe. One of them said harshly, "We don't think it is wise to bring that boy of yours out here. It is bad luck to have the likes of him in our village. We doubt if the Lagoon Spirit is pleased to have him sitting here as well! You must keep him in your house."

Then there was that awful night. The moon was a shining pearl in the sky and everything was awash with its light. As the drums in the village boomed and echoed, the message was clear to Sosu: Come out to play! Come out to play!

Without thinking, Sosu dragged himself out of the house. While he was moving towards the sound of the drums, a girl appeared from nowhere. Startled by Sosu, she screamed so loudly that people came running to the scene. Apparently, the young girl had thought Sosu was a spirit!

The next morning, Fusa tried hard to cheer him up. Whenever Sosu was alone, the dog would insist that they play. That did not help. All Sosu did was throw a corncob as far as he could. The dog then ran and leapt into the air to catch it before it touched the ground!

So often while Fusa still hung in the air, feet, tail and all, Sosu whistled for the chickens to come. He enjoyed watching them – perhaps because there was nothing to envy about them!

Everyday, Sosu would prepare lunch for Fafa and Bubu when they returned from school, although Ma would have to set things up ahead of time. Fafa and Bubu would tell him every new thing they had learned at school, which is how Sosu too learned to read and write.

In the evenings, though, when everybody was home, it was a different matter. It seemed then that those with good legs should do everything.

But one day, all of that changed. Well, nearly. It was a
Monday, so everyone was away as usual. The men were
out fishing, the women were hard at work on their gardens,
and the children were at school in the neighboring village.

Suddenly, Fusa became restless. He began to whimper
and bark while a sudden darkness fell like a blanket across
the sky.

The chickens stopped scratching and jumped onto their
perch in the rafters and remained still, except for their quiet
clucks and cackles. The usual lazy yawn of the sea turned
into an angry howl. The coconut leaves flapped and
rustled, swaying desperately in the wind. The surf boomed
and thundered as it crashed heavily against the sands!

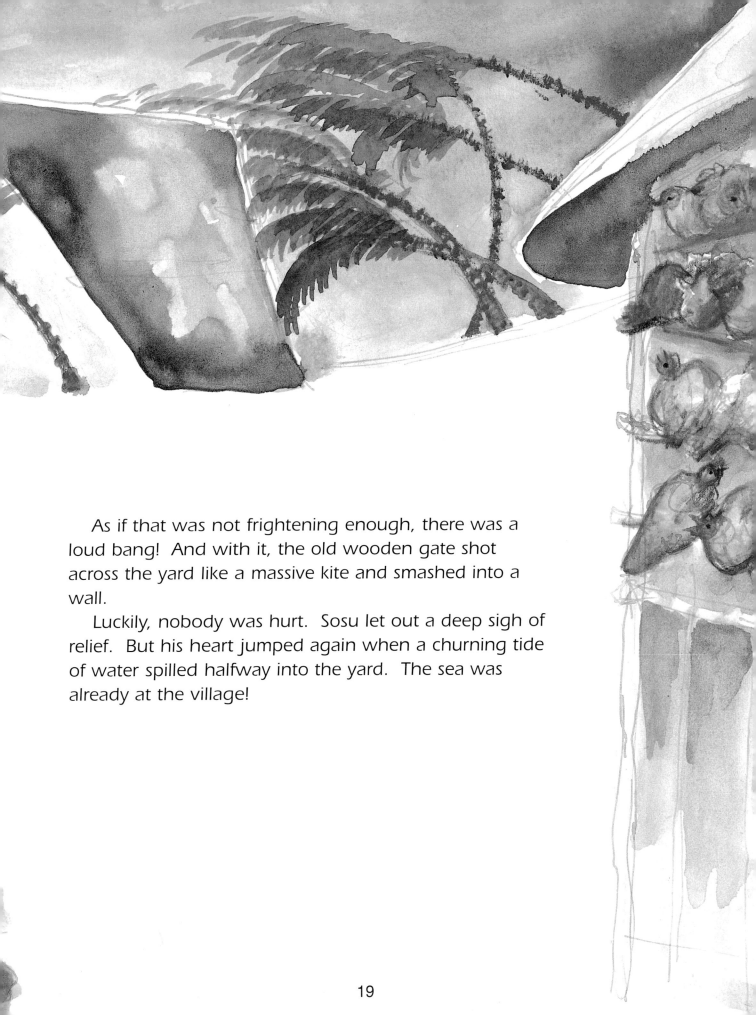

As if that was not frightening enough, there was a loud bang! And with it, the old wooden gate shot across the yard like a massive kite and smashed into a wall.

Luckily, nobody was hurt. Sosu let out a deep sigh of relief. But his heart jumped again when a churning tide of water spilled halfway into the yard. The sea was already at the village!

Something had to be done! And fast! But what could he do? The only other people in the village were those too old or too young or too weak to do anything. They could all be trapped and drowned if the sea continued to rise!

Sosu tried to shout, but he could hardly hear his own voice. He stopped for a moment to think. There must be something useful that even he could do. But what was it? Perhaps Fusa was aware of what Sosu was thinking because he had stopped whimpering. Now he was relaxed, and there was a knowing and reassuring look in his eyes.

That was the moment Sosu got his idea. "The drums!" he said loudly. He would have to try to reach the drum shed behind the chief's house. But with the storm, it would be dangerous even for a person with good legs!

He could think only of the many people and animals that were in serious danger. The look in Fusa's eyes told Sosu, "Don't be afraid. We will be all right!"

With Fusa leading the way, Sosu crawled out of the yard and into the storm. The water reached up to the dog's heels. The screaming wind blew and tore at everything in its way.

Fusa would take several cautious steps ahead, stop, turn to look assuredly at Sosu and wag his tail as if to say, "Come on. It's safe. Trust me. We can do it!"

Somehow, he managed to drag himself along, against the howling wind and the churning water. To this day, Sosu does not know where the strength came from to move his frail limbs, or the courage that drove him on.

They reached the drum shed dripping wet, but safe. The shed was dry inside, and Fusa looked very pleased. As the dog stood, wagging its tail, Sosu was faced with another problem. He had never played a real drum before and did not know how to make it talk. But Fusa, as if to say, "There is no time," stood on his hind legs and began to scratch at a medium-size drum with his paws.

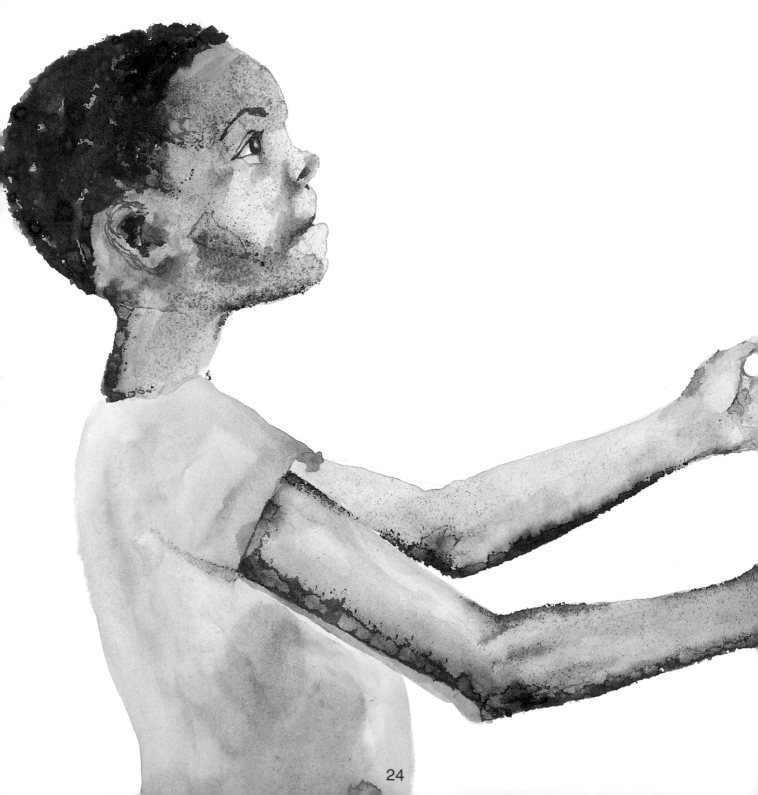

When the top of the drum tilted down towards Sosu, he reached up to stop it from falling on him. After that, he took two sticks in his hands and, striking the top of the drum with one stick, then the other, he began to play.

He played slowly at first, but the storm, the pounding waves, the young children, the sick, the old, the animals, the crashing fences and the snapping trees, all came rushing towards him like moving pictures!

He struck the drum harder and faster until he could hear it above the shrieks and howls of the wind.

belem-belembelem!   bembem-bembem-bembem!
belem-bembem-belem-bembem-belem-bem-bem!
bem-bem-belem!   bem-bem-belem!   bem-bem-belem!

The drum was heard by those at the farthest end of the lagoon, working in the fields. They said, "The drumming is coming from our village. There must be trouble there. Let's go!"

The neighboring village also heard the drum. They too said, "That drumming is from the village on the sandbar. They must be in trouble. Let's go!"

Through the rain and the wind, they all came rushing to Sosu's village.

And what a shock awaited them! Waves as high as roofs were pounding the village! Some houses were so flooded that it took a number of strong men to reach them.

They worked hard, moving from house to house, searching for those who might be trapped.

"We were just in time, thanks to the drummer," they said.

"But who was the drummer?" somebody asked.

Suddenly one of the men shouted, "The boy who can't walk!"
"And his dog!" another added.

"Their house was empty except for the chickens in the rafters."
The anxious men soon found them, thanks to Fusa's sharp ears
and short, excited barks! "The brave drummer and his friend!
Well done! Well done!" Sosu was soon riding on strong shoulders,
with Fusa leaping into the air to reach him!

That was the beginning. Before long, everybody had heard about Sosu. Reporters from newspapers, radio and television came all the way to the village just to see him and talk to him. And of course, they took many pictures of him, his friend Fusa, and his family! He remembers being asked many questions, including why he did something so risky. When asked what he would like the most, he remembers saying something about being able to walk and going to school.

In the weeks that followed, the broken houses and fences were fixed. Best of all the one dusty, bumpy street of the village was scraped even and smooth, and it was extended right to the front gate of Sosu's house.

Then there was the big day in the village square. There was much singing, drumming and dancing; it stopped only when the chief stood up and spoke:

"People of this good village, we are all here today because of one brave little man – and his dog!"

Before he knew what was happening, Sosu was being carried right across the square, as all the people cheered. It was like a dream.

When strong arms finally lowered him down, it was not onto the hard, dusty ground. He was gently placed into a gleaming, new wheelchair!!

Now, he too goes to school, pushed proudly in his wheelchair by the other children of the village. He is just one of the boys of the small village, somewhere between the sea and the lagoon.